WOULD YOU RATHER? FOR

8 YEAR OLD KIDS!

Includes a BONUS
EWW! YUCK! GROSS!
chapter at the end of this book!
HILARIOUS AND FUN!

RatherFunnyPress.com

Books By
RATHER FUNNY PRESS

Would You Rather? For 6 Year Old Kids!
Would You Rather? For 7 Year Old Kids!
Would You Rather? For 8 Year Old Kids!
Would You Rather? For 9 Year Old Kids!
Would You Rather? For 10 Year Old Kids!
Would You Rather? For 11 Year Old Kids!
Would You Rather? For 12 Year Old Kids!
Would You Rather? For Teens!
Would You Rather? Eww! Yuck! Gross!

To see all the latest books by
Rather Funny Press just go to
RatherFunnyPress.com

RatherFunnyPress.com

YOUR FREE SURPRISE GIFT!

Details on the last page of this book!
A brand new free joke book
just for you.
Check it out! Laughter awaits!

RatherFunnyPress.com

HOW TO PLAY

This easy to play game is a ton of fun!
Have 2 or more players.
The first reader will choose a 'Would You Rather?'
from the book and read it aloud.
The other player(s) then choose which scenario
they would prefer and why.
You can't say 'neither' or 'none'.
You must choose one and explain why.
Then the book is passed to the next person
and the game continues!

The main rule is have fun, laugh and enjoy
spending time with your friends and family.
Let the fun begin!

ATTENTION!

All the scenarios and choices in this book are
fictional and meant to be about using your
imagination, having a ton of fun and enjoying this
game with your friends and family.
Obviously, DO NOT ATTEMPT any of these
scenarios in real life.

RatherFunnyPress.com

WOULD YOU RATHER...

RIDE IN A HOT AIR BALLOON

OR

RIDE IN A HOVERCRAFT?

LOSE THE ABILITY TO READ

OR

LOSE THE ABILITY TO SPEAK?

WOULD YOU RATHER...

BATTLE 30 ELEPHANTS THE SIZE OF A CHICKEN

OR

ONE CHICKEN THE SIZE OF AN ELEPHANT?

ALWAYS BE REALLY EARLY EVERYWHERE YOU GO

OR

ALWAYS BE 20 MINUTES LATE?

WOULD YOU RATHER...

ONLY BE ABLE TO DRINK
FRUIT JUICE

OR

ONLY BE ABLE TO DRINK SODA?

HAVE EDIBLE SPAGHETTI HAIR
THAT REGROWS EVERY NIGHT

OR

SWEAT MAPLE SYRUP?

WOULD YOU RATHER...

WEAR THE SAME THING EVERY DAY

OR

NEVER WEAR THE SAME CLOTHES TWICE?

HAVE HANDS INSTEAD OF FEET

OR

FEET INSTEAD OF HANDS?

WOULD YOU RATHER...

LIVE IN A TREEHOUSE

OR

LIVE ON A BOAT?

HAVE SUPER LONG EXTENDING LEGS

OR

SUPER LONG EXTENDING ARMS?

WOULD YOU RATHER...

INSTANTLY BECOME A
GROWN UP

OR

STAY THE AGE YOU ARE NOW
FOR ANOTHER TWO YEARS?

SKYDIVE

OR

BUNGEE JUMP?

WOULD YOU RATHER...

START A COLONY ON
ANOTHER PLANET

OR

BE THE LEADER OF A SMALL
COUNTRY ON EARTH?

HAVE A MAGIC CARPET
THAT FLIES

OR

A SEE-THROUGH SUBMARINE?

WOULD YOU RATHER...

BE ABLE TO TELEPORT ANYWHERE

OR

BE ABLE TO READ MINDS?

SEE ONLY IN BLACK AND WHITE

OR

HAVE CONSTANT RINGING IN YOUR EARS?

WOULD YOU RATHER...

HAVE THE CHANCE TO DESIGN
A NEW TOY

OR

CREATE A NEW TV SHOW?

BE BULLETPROOF

OR

BE ABLE TO SURVIVE FALLS
FROM ANY HEIGHT?

WOULD YOU RATHER...

DO SCHOOL WORK IN A GROUP

OR

BY YOURSELF?

IT BE WARM AND RAINING

OR

COLD AND SNOWING?

WOULD YOU RATHER...

LIVE IN A WORLD WITH
NO CHOCOLATE

OR

LIVE IN A WORLD WITH
NO PIZZA?

PLAY HIDE AND SEEK

OR

PLAY DODGEBALL?

WOULD YOU RATHER...

NEVER SEE ANOTHER MOVIE

OR

NEVER HEAR ANOTHER SONG?

HAVE HAIR THAT GROWS AT ONE FOOT A DAY

OR

BE COMPLETELY BALD?

WOULD YOU RATHER...

NEVER BE STUCK IN
TRAFFIC AGAIN

OR

NEVER GET ANOTHER
COLD?

HAVE A HORSE'S TAIL

OR

HAVE A UNICORN HORN?

WOULD YOU RATHER...

HAVE AN EXTRA EYE ON YOUR FOREHEAD

OR

AN EXTRA EYE ON THE BACK OF YOUR HEAD?

EAT SOME WEEDS TOPPED WITH MELTED CHOCOLATE

OR

EAT A CHOCOLATE BAR COATED IN MUD?

WOULD YOU RATHER...

WALK 25 MILES

OR

SWIM 10 MILES?

SPEND A WEEK IN PARIS

OR

SPEND TWO DAYS AT DISNEYLAND?

WOULD YOU RATHER...

ONLY EAT RICE

OR

ONLY EAT BREAD?

BE ALLERGIC TO
CHOCOLATE

OR

BE ALLERGIC TO
SODA?

WOULD YOU RATHER...

HAVE SUPER SENSITIVE TASTE

OR

SUPER SENSITIVE HEARING?

HAVE A PINOCCHIO NOSE

OR

HAVE DUMBO EARS?

WOULD YOU RATHER...

BE ABLE TO
SLOW DOWN TIME

OR

RUN INCREDIBLY FAST?

FLY ANYWHERE YOU WANTED
FOR FREE

OR

EAT IN ANY RESTAURANT
YOU WANTED FOR FREE?

WOULD YOU RATHER...

BE COVERED IN FUR

OR

COVERED IN SCALES?

BE ABLE TO SHRINK DOWN
TO THE SIZE OF AN ANT

OR

GROW TO THE SIZE OF A
TWO STORY BUILDING?

WOULD YOU RATHER...

WIN AN OLYMPIC GOLD MEDAL

OR

AN ACADEMY AWARD?

HAVE A PIG NOSE

OR

A MONKEY FACE?

WOULD YOU RATHER...

HAVE INFINITE PANCAKES BUT YOU CAN'T STOP EATING THEM

OR

EVERY TIME YOU EAT CANDY YOU SHRINK 1 INCH?

RIDE A GIANT ANT

OR

RIDE A HUGE LIZARD?

WOULD YOU RATHER...

TRAVEL THE WORLD FOR A YEAR
ALL EXPENSES PAID

OR

HAVE $20,000 TO SPEND ON
WHATEVER YOU WANT?

BE UNABLE TO MOVE YOUR BODY
EVERY TIME IT RAINS

OR

NOT BE ABLE TO STOP MOVING
WHILE THE SUN IS OUT?

WOULD YOU RATHER...

HAVE CONSTANTLY DRY EYES

OR

A CONSTANT RUNNY NOSE?

BE AN AVENGER

OR

A RACE CAR DRIVER?

WOULD YOU RATHER...

BE A SUPERHERO
NOBODY KNOWS ABOUT

OR

A WORLD FAMOUS VILLAIN?

LIVE IN AN AMUSEMENT PARK

OR

LIVE IN A CIRCUS?

WOULD YOU RATHER...

HAVE EYES THAT CHANGE COLOR DEPENDING ON YOUR MOOD

OR

HAIR THAT CHANGES COLOR DEPENDING ON THE WEATHER?

DRINK ALL YOUR FOOD FROM A BABY BOTTLE

OR

WEAR VISIBLE DIAPERS FOR THE REST OF YOUR LIFE?

WOULD YOU RATHER...

HAVE AN ELEPHANT'S TRUNK FOR A NOSE

OR

A SNAKE'S TONGUE?

BE A WIZARD

OR

A SUPERHERO?

WOULD YOU RATHER...

HAVE A PERSONAL
LIFE-SIZED ROBOT

OR

A JETPACK?

HAVE CHAPPED LIPS THAT
NEVER HEAL

OR

TERRIBLE DANDRUFF?

WOULD YOU RATHER...

HAVE A GIANT, MAGIC BALL PIT

OR

A SLIDE THAT GOES FROM YOUR ROOF TO THE GROUND?

BE ABLE TO JUMP OVER A TREE

OR

BE ABLE TO THROW A TREE?

WOULD YOU RATHER...

LOSE BOTH YOUR FEET

OR

BOTH YOUR HANDS?

LIVE A SHORT LIFE AND
BE RICH

OR

HAVE A LONG LIFE AND
BE POOR?

WOULD YOU RATHER...

LIVE IN A CAVE

OR

LIVE IN A TREE HOUSE?

EAT A SPOONFUL OF SALT

OR

EAT A SPOONFUL OF PEPPER?

WOULD YOU RATHER...

RIDE A BULL AT THE RODEO
FOR 30 SECONDS

OR

SWIM WITH A SHARK FOR
10 SECONDS?

LICK A PUBLIC
BATHROOM FLOOR

OR

LICK A PUBLIC BATHROOM
TAP HANDLE?

WOULD YOU RATHER...

SLEEP IN A GARBAGE BIN FOR A WEEK

OR

IN A PIGSTY FOR 2 NIGHTS?

GET BITTEN BY A SPIDER ONCE A MONTH FOR A YEAR

OR

STUNG BY A BEE ONCE A DAY FOR A YEAR?

WOULD YOU RATHER...

EVERYTHING IN YOUR HOUSE BE ONE COLOR

OR

EVERY SINGLE WALL AND DOOR BE A DIFFERENT COLOR?

HAVE A PORTAL TO THE ARCADE

OR

HAVE A PORTAL TO THE PLAYGROUND?

WOULD YOU RATHER...

HAVE A THREE FEET
LONG NECK

OR

EARS AS BIG AS AN
ELEPHANT?

BE ATTACKED BY
DINOSAURS

OR

BE ATTACKED BY ALIENS?

WOULD YOU RATHER...

BE ABLE TO MOVE SILENTLY
LIKE A NINJA

OR

HAVE AN INCREDIBLY LOUD
AND SCARY VOICE?

BE ABLE TO BREATHE
UNDERWATER

OR

BE INVISIBLE?

WOULD YOU RATHER...

BE ABLE TO FLY FOR
ONE DAY

OR

BE SUPER STRONG FOR
A WEEK?

NEVER EAT CANDY
EVER AGAIN

OR

NEVER WATCH TV
EVER AGAIN?

WOULD YOU RATHER...

WALK ACROSS A MILE OF HOT COALS

OR

WALK ACROSS A MILE OF LEGOS?

VACATION IN AUSTRALIA

OR

VACATION IN JAPAN?

WOULD YOU RATHER...

GO SNORKELING ON
A REEF

OR

CAMPING BY A LAKE?

ONLY BE ABLE TO USE
A FORK

OR

ONLY BE ABLE TO USE
A SPOON?

WOULD YOU RATHER...

BE ABLE TO TYPE AND TEXT
VERY FAST

OR

READ REALLY QUICKLY?

BE A POLICE OFFICER WITH
A SQUEAKY VOICE

OR

A POLICE OFFICER WITH THE
APPEARANCE OF AN
8 YEAR OLD?

WOULD YOU RATHER...

SPEND A WEEK IN SPACE

OR

SPEND A WEEK ON THE BOTTOM OF THE OCEAN?

BE IN JAIL FOR A YEAR

OR

LOSE A YEAR OFF YOUR LIFE?

WOULD YOU RATHER...

WEAR CLOWN SHOES
EVERY DAY

OR

A CLOWN WIG EVERY DAY?

SNORT A SPOON OF MUSTARD
UP YOUR NOSE

OR

EAT A WHOLE CUP OF SUGAR?

WOULD YOU RATHER...

HAVE A NEVER-ENDING SUPPLY OF CHOCOLATE

OR

A NEVER-ENDING SUPPLY OF ICE CREAM?

BE A POLICE OFFICER

OR

A FIREFIGHTER?

WOULD YOU RATHER...

BE ABLE TO RUN
INCREDIBLY FAST

OR

JUMP INCREDIBLY HIGH?

BE ABLE TO PERFECTLY IMITATE
ANY VOICE YOU HEARD

OR

BE ABLE TO REMEMBER
EVERYTHING YOU'VE EVER
SEEN OR HEARD?

WOULD YOU RATHER...

BE REALLY GOOD AT MATH

OR

REALLY GOOD AT SPORTS?

RIDE A VERY BIG HORSE

OR

A VERY SMALL PONY?

WOULD YOU RATHER...

HAVE A PET CAT THAT CAN SPEAK ENGLISH

OR

A PET DOG THAT IS BIG ENOUGH TO RIDE?

BE A DOCTOR

OR

A TEACHER?

WOULD YOU RATHER...

LIVE IN A HOUSE SHAPED
LIKE A CIRCLE

OR

A HOUSE SHAPED LIKE
A TRIANGLE?

BE A FAMOUS ARTIST

OR

AN INCREDIBLE SINGER?

WOULD YOU RATHER...

NEVER HAVE ANY
HOMEWORK

OR

BE PAID $5 PER HOUR FOR
DOING YOUR HOMEWORK?

BE 6 FEET TALL AND
REALLY WEAK

OR

4 FEET TALL AND
REALLY STRONG?

WOULD YOU RATHER...

BE ABLE TO CREATE
A NEW HOLIDAY

OR

CREATE A NEW SPORT?

HAVE YOUR ROOM REDECORATED
HOWEVER YOU WANT

OR

TEN TOYS OF YOUR CHOICE?

WOULD YOU RATHER...

HAVE A PET GIRAFFE

OR

A PET LLAMA?

BE AN AMAZING DANCER

OR

AN AMAZING SINGER?

WOULD YOU RATHER...

BE ALONE FOR THE REST
OF YOUR LIFE

OR

ALWAYS BE SURROUNDED BY
ANNOYING PEOPLE?

GO SWIMMING IN A RIVER
OF CHOCOLATE

OR

DIVE INTO A POOL OF SODA?

WOULD YOU RATHER...

NOT BE ABLE TO OPEN ANY CLOSED DOORS

OR

CLOSE ANY OPEN DOORS?

HAVE A PET WORM THAT LIVED IN YOUR NOSE

OR

A PET FLY THAT LIVED IN YOUR EAR?

WOULD YOU RATHER...

BE AN ASTRONAUT

OR

A ROBOT?

ONLY BE ABLE TO WALK
ON ALL FOURS

OR

ONLY BE ABLE TO WALK
SIDEWAYS LIKE A CRAB?

WOULD YOU RATHER...

EAT AN APPLE

OR

AN ORANGE?

NEVER BE ABLE TO DRINK
SODA AGAIN

OR

ONLY BE ABLE TO DRINK SODA
AND NOTHING ELSE?

WOULD YOU RATHER...

EAT CHOCOLATE
TACOS

OR

CHOCOLATE PIZZA?

TRAIN A DINOSAUR
SIZED CHICKEN

OR

TRAIN A CHICKEN
SIZED DINOSAUR?

WOULD YOU RATHER...

NEVER CUT YOUR HAIR AGAIN

OR

NEVER SHOWER AGAIN?

HAVE TO SKIP INSTEAD OF WALK

OR

RUN REALLY FAST EVERYWHERE YOU GO?

WOULD YOU RATHER...

BE LOCKED IN A ROOM THAT IS CONSTANTLY DARK FOR A WEEK

OR

A ROOM THAT IS CONSTANTLY BRIGHT FOR A WEEK?

SEE A FIREWORK DISPLAY

OR

SEE A CIRCUS PERFORMANCE?

WOULD YOU RATHER...

BE A JEDI WITHOUT
A LIGHTSABER

OR

A WIZARD WITHOUT A WAND?

EAT ONLY FRUIT

OR

ONLY VEGETABLES?

WOULD YOU RATHER...

HAVE A WATER SLIDE WITH A HEATED POOL IN YOUR HOUSE

OR

A BOWLING ALLEY IN YOUR HOUSE?

HAVE NO FINGERS

OR

NO EARS?

WOULD YOU RATHER...

BE ALLERGIC TO
HASH BROWNS

OR

ALLERGIC TO CANDY?

BE THE BEST IN THE WORLD
AT CLIMBING TREES

OR

THE BEST IN THE WORLD AT
JUMPING ROPE?

WOULD YOU RATHER...

EAT 50 CHICKEN NUGGETS

OR

4 BIG MACS?

HAVE A TINY HEAD COMPARED TO YOUR BODY

OR

HAVE A FURRY FACE?

WOULD YOU RATHER...

HAVE A NEW SILLY HAT APPEAR IN YOUR CLOSET EVERY MORNING

OR

A NEW PAIR OF SHOES APPEAR IN YOUR CLOSET ONCE A WEEK?

LIVE IN THE HARRY POTTER WORLD

OR

THE STAR WARS WORLD?

WOULD YOU RATHER...

RIDE IN AN ARMY TANK

OR

RIDE IN A HOT AIR BALLOON?

NOT BE ABLE TO
STOP DANCING

OR

NOT BE ABLE TO
STOP SINGING?

WOULD YOU RATHER...

WRESTLE A GIANT SNAKE

OR

WRESTLE A GIANT SPIDER?

GO TO THE BEACH
WHENEVER YOU WANT

OR

GO TO THE SNOW
WHENEVER YOU WANT?

WOULD YOU RATHER...

HAVE TO READ ALOUD
EVERY WORD YOU READ

OR

SING EVERYTHING YOU
SAY OUT LOUD?

ONLY EAT
BREAKFAST CEREAL

OR

ONLY EAT PASTA?

WOULD YOU RATHER...

EAT A BOWL OF SPAGHETTI NOODLES WITHOUT SAUCE

OR

A BOWL OF SPAGHETTI SAUCE WITHOUT NOODLES?

DRINK EVERY MEAL AS A SMOOTHIE

OR

NEVER BE ABLE TO EAT FOOD THAT HAS BEEN COOKED?

WOULD YOU RATHER...

WRESTLE AN ALLIGATOR
ONE TIME

OR

HAVE TO WEAR ONLY PINK
FOR A YEAR?

HAVE ALL DOGS TRY TO ATTACK
YOU WHEN THEY SEE YOU

OR

ALL BIRDS TRY TO ATTACK YOU
WHEN THEY SEE YOU?

WOULD YOU RATHER...

NEVER BE ABLE TO EAT MEAT

OR

NEVER BE ABLE TO
EAT VEGETABLES?

HAVE ONE HUGE EYEBROW
ACROSS YOUR FOREHEAD

OR

NO EYEBROWS AT ALL?

WOULD YOU RATHER...

HAVE REALLY, REALLY LONG FINGERS

OR

REALLY, REALLY LONG TOES?

EAT SNAIL FLAVORED ICE CREAM

OR

DRINK ROTTEN WORM FLAVORED SODA?

WOULD YOU RATHER...

HAVE HUGE ARMS
AND WEAK LEGS

OR

HAVE HUGE LEGS
AND WEAK ARMS?

ALWAYS HAVE MUD
ON YOUR SHOES

OR

ALWAYS HAVE A PEBBLE
IN YOUR SHOE?

WOULD YOU RATHER...

HOLD A SNAKE

OR

KISS A JELLYFISH?

PAINT YOUR HOUSE USING YOUR HAND AS A PAINTBRUSH

OR

MOW THE LAWN BY EATING THE GRASS?

WOULD YOU RATHER...

? **?**

EAT A ROTTEN BANANA

OR

EAT A CUP FULL OF GRASS?

? **?** **?**

GIVE UP WATCHING TV AND
MOVIES FOR A YEAR

OR

GIVE UP PLAYING
VIDEO GAMES FOR A YEAR?

? **?**

WOULD YOU RATHER...

GET A FREE APPETIZER
WITH EVERY MEAL

OR

GET A FREE DESSERT
WITH EVERY MEAL?

ONLY WEAR ONE COLOR
EACH DAY

OR

HAVE TO WEAR SEVEN
COLORS EACH DAY?

WOULD YOU RATHER...

DANCE IN FRONT OF
1,000 PEOPLE

OR

SING IN FRONT OF
1,000 PEOPLE?

HAVE UNLIMITED COOKIES THAT
YOU CAN NEVER STOP EATING

OR

NEVER EAT A COOKIE AGAIN?

WOULD YOU RATHER...

TAKE A SIZZLING HOT SHOWER

OR

TAKE A FREEZING COLD SHOWER?

LIVE IN AUSTRALIA

OR

LIVE IN MEXICO?

WOULD YOU RATHER...

BE ALLERGIC TO CANDY

OR

ALLERGIC TO POPCORN?

MEET YOUR
FAVORITE CELEBRITY

OR

BE ON A TV SHOW?

WOULD YOU RATHER...

HAVE A TAIL THAT CAN'T GRAB THINGS

OR

WINGS THAT CAN'T FLY?

HAVE AN AIR HOCKEY TABLE

OR

A PINBALL MACHINE?

WOULD YOU RATHER...

TEACH HISTORY

OR

TEACH MATH?

BE ABLE TO JUMP AS FAR AS A KANGAROO

OR

HOLD YOUR BREATH AS LONG AS A WHALE?

WOULD YOU RATHER...

BE BATMAN

OR

IRON MAN?

HAVE A SLIPPERY SLIDE
TO GET DOWNSTAIRS

OR

HAVE A TRAMPOLINE
TO GET UPSTAIRS?

WOULD YOU RATHER...

HAVE 1,000 COCKROACHES IN YOUR BEDROOM

OR

HAVE A BATH WITH 1,000 WRIGGLING WORMS?

MEET YOUR FUTURE SELF

OR

MEET YOUR FUTURE KIDS?

WOULD YOU RATHER...

DO YOUR OWN STUNTS IN
AN ACTION MOVIE

OR

HAVE A STUNT PERSON
DO THEM FOR YOU?

BE A GHOST

OR

A VAMPIRE?

WOULD YOU RATHER...

HOLD A SNAKE
FOR 2 HOURS

OR

4 REALLY BIG SPIDERS
FOR 1 HOUR?

ONLY BE ABLE TO JUMP
EVERYWHERE YOU GO

OR

ONLY BE ABLE TO WALK
ON YOUR HANDS?

WOULD YOU RATHER...

SWAP YOUR FEET FOR
ROLLER SKATES

OR

KEEP YOUR FEET
AS THEY ARE?

NOT BE ABLE TO SIT

OR

NOT BE ABLE TO STAND?

WOULD YOU RATHER...

STAY IN SCHOOL FOR
THE NEXT 20 YEARS

OR

LEAVE SCHOOL AFTER
FIFTH GRADE?

HAVE YOUR CURRENT PET LIVE
AS LONG AS YOU DO

OR

BRING A PAST PET
BACK TO LIFE?

WOULD YOU RATHER...

NOT BE ABLE TO TASTE

OR

NOT BE ABLE TO SMELL?

FIGHT THREE BULLS
AT THE SAME TIME

OR

FIGHT TEN BULLS
ONE AT A TIME?

WOULD YOU RATHER...

WEAR CLOWN MAKEUP
EVERY DAY FOR A YEAR

OR

WEAR A TUTU EVERY DAY
FOR A YEAR?

NOT BE ABLE TO READ

OR

NOT BE ABLE TO SPEAK?

WOULD YOU RATHER...

HAVE A
SPACE INVADERS MACHINE

OR

A PAC-MAN MACHINE?

RIDE A DONKEY TO SCHOOL

OR

A GIRAFFE TO SCHOOL?

WOULD YOU RATHER...

HAVE CHEWING GUM
STUCK IN YOUR HAIR

OR

CHEWING GUM STUCK
UP YOUR NOSE?

HAVE GRAVITY TURN OFF
FOR A DAY

OR

HAVE THE SUN TURN OFF
FOR A WEEK?

WOULD YOU RATHER...

YELL AT THE TOP OF YOUR VOICE EVERY TIME YOU SPOKE

OR

NEVER SPEAK EVER AGAIN?

RANDOMLY TURN INTO A FROG FOR A DAY ONCE A MONTH

OR

RANDOMLY TURN INTO A BIRD FOR A DAY ONCE EVERY WEEK?

WOULD YOU RATHER...

BE ABLE TO SEE THROUGH
SOLID WALLS

OR

HEAR PEOPLE TALKING
A MILE AWAY?

EAT A SMALL CAN OF
CAT FOOD

OR

EAT TWO ROTTEN TOMATOES?

WOULD YOU RATHER...

ONLY EAT KFC FOR A MONTH

OR

ONLY EAT MCDONALDS
FOR A MONTH?

HAVE A MAGICAL
FLYING CARPET

OR

A CAR THAT CAN
DRIVE UNDERWATER?

WOULD YOU RATHER...

NEVER BE ABLE TO EAT WARM FOOD AGAIN

OR

NEVER BE ABLE TO EAT COLD FOOD AGAIN?

HAVE A COMPLETELY AUTOMATED HOME

OR

A SELF-DRIVING CAR?

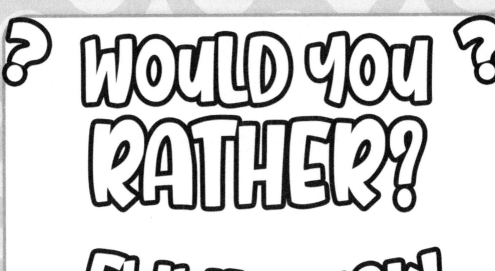

WOULD YOU RATHER?

EWW! YUCK! GROSS!

This way to crazy, ridiculous
and downright hilarious
'Would You Rathers?!'

WARNING!

These are Eww! These are Yuck! These
are Gross! And they are really funny!
Laughter awaits!

RatherFunnyPress.com

WOULD YOU RATHER...

FART LOUDLY IN
A QUIET LIBRARY

OR

BARF ON YOUR
TEACHER'S SHOES?

FIND A POO IN THE BATHTUB

OR

FIND A POO IN THE SHOWER?

WOULD YOU RATHER...

HAVE MAGGOTS LIVING
IN YOUR HAIR

OR

HAVE WORMS LIVING IN YOUR
EARS AND NOSE?

PEE YOUR PANTS
WHEN YOU LAUGH

OR

PEE YOUR PANTS
WHEN YOU CRY?

WOULD YOU RATHER...

HAVE A BATH IN 5 GALLONS
OF HOT CHILLI SAUCE

OR

5 GALLONS OF VINEGAR?

SMELL YOUR
BEST FRIEND'S BREATH

OR

HAVE THEM SMELL
YOUR BREATH?

WOULD YOU RATHER...

SIT IN A HOT TUB FULL OF
SNAILS AND WORMS

OR

SWIM IN A POOL FULL OF
ROTTEN FISH?

EAT A CHUNK OF
SKUNK HAIR

OR

DRINK A GLASS OF
STINKY SWEAT?

WOULD YOU RATHER...

EAT LIVE MAGGOTS

OR

POOP OUT LIVE MAGGOTS?

HAVE PEPPER GET
INTO YOUR EYES

OR

BREATHE PEPPER
INTO YOUR NOSE?

WOULD YOU RATHER...

SNIFF A CAT'S BUTT

OR

SNIFF A DOG'S BUTT?

SMELL YOUR
FRIEND'S BREATH

OR

SMELL YOUR
FRIEND'S FART?

WOULD YOU RATHER...

LICK THE ARMPIT OF
A SWEATY HIKER

OR

LICK THE EARWAX OF
AN OLD MAN?

DO ONE REALLY BIG POO
ONCE A WEEK

OR

LOTS OF LITTLE POOS
FIVE TIMES A DAY?

WOULD YOU RATHER...

LICK THE CLASSROOM FLOOR

OR

LICK THE BOTTOM OF YOUR TEACHER'S SHOE?

HAVE 5 SCORPIONS CRAWL ALL OVER YOU

OR

HAVE A BUCKET OF MAGGOTS DROPPED ON YOU FROM ABOVE?

WOULD YOU RATHER...

EAT A ROTTEN APPLE

OR

LICK A SWEATY
BODYBUILDER'S UNDERPANTS?

BRUSH YOUR TEETH WITH FART
FLAVORED TOOTHPASTE

OR

WASH YOUR HAIR WITH
ROTTEN FISH GUTS?

WOULD YOU RATHER...

BURP IN FRONT OF
YOUR TEACHER

OR

FART LOUDLY ON A
FIRST DATE?

DO REALLY LOUD FARTS THAT
DIDN'T SMELL AT ALL

OR

SILENT FARTS THAT
SMELT REALLY BAD?

THANKS A BUNCH!

For reading our book!
We hope you have enjoyed these
'WOULD YOU RATHER?'
scenarios as much as we did as we were
putting this book together.
If you could possibly leave a review of our
book we would really appreciate it. ☺

To see all our latest books or leave a review
just go to
RatherFunnyPress.com
Once again, thanks so much for reading!

P.S. If you enjoyed the bonus chapter,
EWW! YUCK! GROSS!
you can always check out our brand new book,

WOULD YOU RATHER?
EWW! YUCK! GROSS!
for hundreds of brand new, crazy and ridiculous
scenarios that are sure to get the kids rolling on the
floor with laughter!
Just go to:
RatherFunnyPress.com
Thanks again! ☺

YOUR FREE SURPRISE GIFT!

HILARIOUS JOKES FOR CLEVER KIDS!

RATHER FUNNY PRESS

To grab your free copy of this brand new, hilarious Joke Book, just go to:

go.RatherFunnyPress.com

Enjoy!

RatherFunnyPress.com

Printed in Great Britain
by Amazon

75280015R00066